Yankee Doodle

For Alexandra,
born on the Fourth of July
—P.G.

ISBN 0-439-44530-2

12 11 10 9 8 7 6 5 4 3 2 1   2 3 4 5 6 7/0

Printed in the U.S.A.
First printing, October 2002

Yankee Doodle

Illustrated by Patti Goodnow

SCHOLASTIC INC.

New York Toronto London Auckland Sydney
Mexico City New Delhi Hong Kong Buenos Aires

Yankee Doodle went to town,

Riding on a pony.

Stuck a feather in his cap
And called it macaroni.

Yankee Doodle, keep it up.

Yankee Doodle dandy,

Mind the music and the step,

And with the girls be handy.

Yankee Doodle

Yan–kee Doo–dle went to town, Ri- ding on a po — ny.

Stuck a feath–er in his cap And called it mac–a ro — ni.

Yan–kee Doo–dle, keep it up. Yan–kee Doo–dle dan – dy,

Mind the mu – sic and the step, And with the girls be han – dy .